For Dedria and Jill, who got me started.
Honoring the memory of my mother, Edith Erickson Wilbur (1919-2009), and her prize-winning Victory Garden.

Helen

To my daughter Catherine, who always inspires me with her love of life and of people.

Robert

★   ★   ★

Sleeping Bear Press wishes to gratefully acknowledge the D. Landreth Seed Company
for permitting the use of their colorful seed packets depicted on the endpapers of this book.
(D. Landreth Seed Company, 60 East High Street, Building #4,
New Freedom, Pennsylvania 17349 | www.landrethseeds.com)

Photograph of Victory Gardeners in the afterword from
Library of Congress Prints and Photographs Division
Washington, D.C. 20504
Photograph by Alfred Palmer and /or Howard Hollem for the
U.S. Office of Emergency Management, taken between 1942-1943.
Control Number 2004673061.

Sleeping Bear Press
315 E. Eisenhower Parkway, Suite 200
Ann Arbor, MI 48108
www.sleepingbearpress.com

© 2010 Sleeping Bear Press is an imprint of Gale, a part of Cengage Learning.

Library of Congress Cataloging-in-Publication Data

Wilbur, Helen L., 1948-
Lily's victory garden / written by Helen L. Wilbur ; illustrated by Robert Gantt Steele. —1st ed.
p. cm. — (Tales of young Americans)
Summary: Lily gets permission to plant a Victory Garden at a house where the Bishops'
son has died in the war, and slowly the garden helps Mrs. Bishop recover from her grief.
ISBN 978-1-58536-450-3
1. World War, 1939-1945—United States—Juvenile fiction. [1. World War, 1939-1945—United
States—Fiction. 2. Victory gardens—Fiction. 3. Gardens—Fiction. 4. Gardening—Fiction.]
I. Steele, Robert Gantt, ill. II. Title.
PZ7.W6413Li 2010
[E]—dc22   2009036937
Printed by China Translation & Printing Services Limited, Guangdong Province, China. 1st printing. 12/2009

Lily's
VICTORY ★ GARDEN

Written by HELEN L. WILBUR

Illustrated by ROBERT GANTT STEELE

SLEEPING BEAR PRESS
TALES of YOUNG AMERICANS SERIES

My brother Jack and I go every Saturday to collect tin cans and scrap for the war effort. We also pick up the full cans of grease the army uses to make bombs and bullets. Although how they make bullets out of bacon drippings, I have never figured out.

This is Jack's paper route so all the folks know him. And our big, brown dog, Thunder.

*　*　*

We always collect last from the Bishops' place. It's the biggest house with the biggest yard and a gold star service flag in the front window.

Jack says their son, Ned Bishop, was the first soldier from our town to die in the war. Mr. Bishop walks to the bank every day now to save on rationed gasoline and tires but Mrs. Bishop doesn't go out much any more.

Jack goes up the long gravel drive
to the Bishops' back porch. I wait at
the sidewalk with Thunder. No noise.
No dogs. No bothering Mrs. Bishop.

It's early spring and the crocuses
are just coming up through the hard
earth. There are lots of little purple
and white flowers along the Bishops'
drive. I kneel down for a closer look.
Mrs. Bishop had the best garden ever
and even now the flowers can't stop
coming up on their own.

"Hurry up, Lily, we'll
be late for supper!"

Someday I am going to have a big house with a big garden with every kind of flower all summer long. Right now all I have is a window box overlooking Federal Street from our third floor apartment.

Father says that war is a terrible thing but good for business. He works full time now at the aircraft plant. Mom has a job there, too. We might even be able to save enough money to buy a house after the war, probably not as big as the Bishops', but big enough to have a yard and garden.

After supper every night Father snaps on the radio and we listen to Mr. Gabriel Heatter with the news of the war. Mr. Heatter always says, "Ah, there is good news tonight…" Sometimes the news doesn't seem very good to me.

Then comes the best part of the day when Father and I read the paper together. I sit right next to him in his morris chair and he holds the paper like a little tent with just us in it. First we read the funnies, then we pick one or two stories and I read them out loud.

That's how I find out about almost everything and that's how I decided to have my own Victory Garden.

"The Mayor announced today that the parks council will turn Town Park into Victory Garden plots for citizens to help the war effort by growing vegetables. Plots will be available by lottery and the Garden Club will offer seeds and gardening advice to those…"

With food being rationed, standing in line is something we are all used to now. So I wait in a long line to fill out the forms for the Victory Garden lottery. When I get to the table Mr. Weeks, the Garden Club president, tells me that I have to be 18 years old or part of a club for kids to qualify.

Jack says, "I told you so."

I know where there is a big yard and space for a little garden that won't bother anybody. Jack and my parents will be really mad at me for asking, but I am going to anyway.

The gravel path crunches loudly under my feet and the doorbell chimes deep inside the house. At first it seems that no one is home but Mr. Bishop opens the door. I hand him the Victory Garden leaflet and explain what I want and tell him that I won't be a nuisance. It sounded better when I practiced it in my head.

He looks at the papers and at me. "I'm sorry, Lily, but Mrs. Bishop isn't well and we can't have any disturbance in the yard."

A voice speaks from behind Mr. Bishop. "Edwin, it can't hurt anything, let her have the little kitchen garden that used to be near the garage."

Mr. Bishop isn't happy about this but he puts on his jacket and shows me the small plot of earth. "I don't suppose you have any tools," he says.

"No, sir."

"Come on then." He opens the small back shed; it's dim and dusty but neatly stacked with rakes and hoes.

"You can use these. Now remember, no other children, no noise, no dogs." He shoots a dirty look at Thunder who has snuck up behind me. "And no bothering Mrs. Bishop."

I have the seeds and the instructions but clearing up the dead plants and roots and turning over the soil is harder than the leaflet says.

I go every morning while my parents and Mr. Bishop are working, but the tools are big and there is a lot of work to do before I can plant anything.

But on the fourth morning I come and the whole plot is neatly turned over and shaped into rows— just like the plan I had made on paper and left in the shed. I look around but no one is there and the house is just as shut up and gloomy as ever.

The vegetable seeds have wonderful names like Detroit Dark Red Beets, Kentucky Wonder Beans, Little Marvel Peas, Kleckley's Sweet Watermelon…You know how amazing they are going to be even before they ever start to grow.

Every few days a surprise appears.

One hot morning I find a straw hat sitting on top of the hoe. Another day a little bench sits next to the garden. Sometimes I can see that the soil is wet from the watering can nearby or that those sneaky little weeds that grow overnight have been pulled.

The best surprise, of course, is the tiny green sprouts that begin to push through the earth.

One morning I am inspecting a frilly leaf
to figure out whether it's a vegetable or a weed.

"That's your carrots," a voice says behind me and I jump
a foot. A woman is standing at the corner of the garden.
Her dress hangs on her like it is someone else's.

I have never seen her before but I know who she is.

Mrs. Bishop starts to come for a little while every day.

She knows everything about plants and flowers, even their names in Latin. She tells me that my name in Latin means "blossoming flower."

We walk around the yard and she shows me all the plants and trees, tells me what they are, when they grow, everything. It's like walking downtown and suddenly knowing the names and stories of all the strangers.

One day a downpour catches us. Mrs. Bishop slips and falls in the muddy puddle between the rows of beans as she starts for the porch.

I go to help her get up but Thunder hears us and comes leaping in, knocking me into the mud, too. Mrs. Bishop starts to laugh and Thunder gets excited and barks and, wouldn't you know it, Mr. Bishop in his bank suit appears with his black umbrella around the corner of the garage.

"Emma, Emma!" Mr. Bishop runs to get Mrs. Bishop out of the mud and guides her into the dim house. He is upset and angry and tells me that the gardening is over and not to come any more.

I run home in tears.

Father and Mother know that I have been crying so I have to tell them everything. Worse than being yelled at is that Father says he is disappointed in me. Wanting to help is a fine thing but there are right ways to do it and mine wasn't one of them.

Everyone is quiet at supper. I lie down on my bed with Thunder as it gets dark.

When I hear my parents answer the door and greet Mr. Bishop, I know things have just gotten worse.

"Lily," Mother calls, "please come into the front room."

When I get there, no one looks as mad as I expect. My parents smile at Mr. Bishop, who steps forward.

"Lily, I am sorry about what happened today. I worry so much about Mrs. Bishop that I never noticed how much better she was getting. When I brought her inside, she told me how happy she has been working with you on the Victory Garden. Please come back to us tomorrow," he pauses, "and bring Thunder."

* * *

A garden is a miraculous thing. You plant little seeds, give them water and keep the weeds off them, and you get tomatoes and cucumbers and beans and squash and even really big pumpkins.

Our president, Mr. Franklin D. Roosevelt, says on the radio that we are all one big fighting force, even the children. All these things we do that don't seem like much, well, they all add up. We are friends and neighbors and soldiers and citizens.

✶ ✶ WORLD WAR II *and the* HOME FRONT ✶ ✶

World War II (1941-1945) affected every American, and the U.S. government called upon each citizen to contribute to victory. More than 16 million Americans served in the military, but many more served on the home front to support the effort and ensure victory.

Manufacturing
America, "The Arsenal of Democracy"

Victory depended on using every available resource to build guns, planes, ships, tanks, trucks, and munitions to supply the troops of America and its allies.

This vast manufacturing effort, called mobilization, required that the U.S. government restrict the manufacture of consumer goods like cars and appliances. Automobile companies stopped producing passenger cars on February 10, 1942, in order to make trucks and tanks until the end of the war.

Collecting & Recycling
"Use it up, wear it out, make it do or do without!"

All Americans were urged to conserve and recycle resources. People patched and repaired household appliances, shoes, tires, cars, bicycles, and clothing to make everything last longer. Groups collected metal cans, rubber, and scraps, along with magazines, paper, and wire for recycling. Citizens even collected household grease and fat for the glycerin to be utilized in making explosives. Anything that could be used in the war effort was saved, conserved, and reused.

Rationing

To make sure that the troops received enough supplies and food the U.S. government limited the civilian distribution of meat, sugar, canned goods, gasoline, clothing, and other commodities in a system called rationing. Rationing ensured fair distribution of scarce goods so that all Americans shared equally in the hardships of war.

More than 130 million Americans received ration cards. Each person got a ration card allocating points or stamps to use for food each month and for other items on a monthly or yearly basis.

In other countries shortages were far more severe, with gasoline almost impossible to obtain and food rations barely sufficient to support life.

Service Flags

Starting in World War I, families of men and women serving in war display a banner called a Service Flag in the window of their homes. The Service Flag features a white field bordered in red with a blue star for each son or daughter serving in harm's way and a gold star for a family member killed in active duty.

Newspapers and Radio

World War II took place before most Americans had television sets. People got their news and entertainment from listening to the radio or reading the newspaper. Local movie theaters showed newsreels with weekly war news, along with the feature film presentation.

Victory Gardens

With produce grown on larger farms needed for the troops, the U.S. Department of Agriculture encouraged citizens to plant "Victory Gardens" to ease food shortages and promote healthy eating. More than 20 million Americans answered the call in 1941 through 1943, producing nearly 50% of all the vegetables, fruit, and herbs for civilian consumption in the United States.

This tradition continues today in Community Gardens, bringing people together to beautify their neighborhood and produce nutritious local food.